The Girl Who Never Let Her Mother Brush Her Hair

written and illustrated
by

Doris Irene Rainville

Dedicated to:
Anna whose stubborness inspired this story; Eileen, who told me that I should publish this story; Pam, who encouraged me to publish this story; Alma for her beautiful calligraphy.

Doris Rainville is the only child of Lionel and Rita Rainville and is the mother of Joshua, Celestial, Grace, Anna and Christopher. Her family now includes daughter-in-law Susan and son-in-law Bobby. She has been a single parent since 1986 when her 5th child was a baby. Doris has been a Waldorf Kindergarten teacher since 1991. Her stories have been inspired in order to help her own children and her students work through challenges. It is her hope that these stories will be an inspiration to others.

Illustrations by Doris Rainville
Calligraphy by Alma Rowe
Book Design by Catherine Ardagh

ISBN 0-9744879-0-2
First Edition
2003
Printed in China

Once there were two sisters named Grace and Anna. Grace had long, thick, curly hair and loved it when her mother brushed her hair. Anna, on the other hand, had a very sensitive head, was very stubborn, and did not like to get her hair brushed. One day Anna's mother told her that it was time to brush her hair and Anna said, "Please do not brush my hair mother!" This is when Anna's mother told her the story about a little girl who never let her mother brush her hair, and this is how it went.

Once upon a time there was a little girl named Hannah who lived with her mother in a cottage at the edge of a forest. Every morning after they ate their breakfast, Hannah's mother would ask her to sit down to get her hair brushed. Hannah did not like having her hair brushed and would yell, "No, no, no." Then she would run out of the door and into the forest where she would play all day long.

Playing in the forest was Hannah's favorite thing to do. She loved to climb the tall trees and see how far she could see. For a spell she would sit quietly on one of the trees' branches, listening to the sounds in the forest. With eagle eyes she would look about the forest spying on Mother Nature's creatures, busy with their daily activities. The squirrels and chipmunks scurried about gathering acorns. The deer moved about quietly and gracefully, unless they were startled, in which case they would quickly prance deep into the forest. In the spring, she would watch the birds gather materials to build the nests that would house their eggs.

Day after day, Hannah ran out of her house without getting her hair brushed and day after day, her hair became more and more tangled until it was quite a sight to see.

One fine spring day when Hannah was walking through the forest, the air was filled with birdsong. The birds were busily building their nest, preparing for their young ones, when a mother robin happened to see the little girl's head and thought it would be a fine place to build a nest. In fact, it looked as though there was a nest already started.

The mother bird gathered twigs and pine needles and wove them into Hannah's hair. It became a beautiful nest. Hannah walked proudly through the forest with her new pet robin sitting in the nest, and she felt as though she was the luckiest girl in the whole world.

Within a week, Hannah's robin had laid three eggs in the nest. Hannah moved about very carefully and she was proud to be the guardian of these three special eggs. The mother robin kept the eggs warm until one day, when the eggs started to crack open. This was the most exciting day of Hannah's life, and she loved the baby birds as if they were her own.

The mother robin trusted Hannah to look after the baby birds while she went into the forest to hunt for fat, juicy worms, to feed them. Sometimes the baby birds were so hungry that they would eat the worms all up. Sometimes the worms were so fat that the baby birds could only eat half of them.

Now Hannah not only had three baby birds and a mother bird in her hair, but she also had half eaten, dead worms. And you know what baby birds do after they eat! The situation was not so lovely any more.

Hannah went to her mother and asked, "Mother, will you please help me to wash and brush my hair?" Hannah's mother replied, "Of course dear, but first we must build a house for the birds." They got busy right away and built a lovely birdhouse in the tall oak tree in the back yard. Carefully they put the babies into their new house.

Hannah's mother got the twigs and pine needles out of Hannah's hair. Her hair needed to be washed three times, and then she had to sit still for a very long time while her mother carefully brushed out all of the tangles. It felt so wonderful to have clean, unsnarled hair once again.

From that day forward, before Hannah went out to play in the forest, she would always ask her mother, "Mother, would you please brush my hair for me?" Hannah's mother would always reply, "Yes dear, I would love to."